1 3 5 7 9 10 8 6 4 2

Jonathan Cape, an imprint of Vintage Publishing,
20 Vauxhall Bridge Road,
London SW1V 2SA

Jonathan Cape is part of the Penguin Random House group of companies
whose addresses can be found at global.penguinrandomhouse.com.

Copyright © Kristen Roupenian 2018
Photographs Copyright © Elinor Carucci 2018

Kristen Roupenian has asserted her right to be identified as the author of this
Work in accordance with the Copyright, Designs and Patents Act 1988

'Cat Person' first appeared in the *New Yorker* in December 2017
First published in the UK by Jonathan Cape in 2018

penguin.co.uk/vintage

A CIP catalogue record for this book is available from the British Library

ISBN 9781787331150

Printed and bound in Great Britain by TJ International Ltd, Padstow, Cornwall

Penguin Random House is committed to a sustainable future for our business, our
readers and our planet. This book is made from Forest Stewardship Council® certified paper.

CAT PERSON

Evan almost touches me, 1999

CAT PERSON

KRISTEN ROUPENIAN

JONATHAN CAPE
LONDON

Margot met Robert on a Wednesday night toward the end of her fall semester. She was working behind the concession stand at the artsy movie theatre downtown when he came in and bought a large popcorn and a box of Red Vines.

"That's an . . . unusual choice," she said. "I don't think I've ever actually sold a box of Red Vines before."

CAT PERSON

Flirting with her customers was a habit she'd picked up back when she worked as a barista, and it helped with tips. She didn't earn tips at the movie theatre, but the job was boring otherwise, and she did think that Robert was cute. Not so cute that she would have, say, gone up to him at a party, but cute enough that she could have drummed up an imaginary crush on him if he'd sat across from her during a dull class—though she was pretty sure that he was out of college, in his mid-twenties at least. He was tall, which she liked, and she could see the edge of a tattoo peeking out from beneath the rolled-up sleeve of his shirt. But he was on the heavy side, his beard was a little too long, and his shoulders slumped forward slightly, as though he were protecting something.

Robert did not pick up on her flirtation. Or, if he did, he showed it only by stepping back, as though to make her lean toward him, try a little harder. "Well," he said. "O.K., then." He pocketed his change.

But the next week he came into the movie theatre again, and bought another box of Red Vines. "You're getting better at your job," he told her. "You managed not to insult me this time."

She shrugged. "I'm up for a promotion, so," she said.

After the movie, he came back to her. "Concession-stand girl, give me your phone number," he said, and, surprising herself, she did.

CAT PERSON

From that small exchange about Red Vines, over the next several weeks they built up an elaborate scaffolding of jokes via text, riffs that unfolded and shifted so quickly that she sometimes had a hard time keeping up. He was very clever, and she found that she had to work to impress him. Soon she noticed that when she texted him he usually texted her back right away, but if she took more than a few hours to respond his next message would always be short and wouldn't include a question, so it was up to her to re-initiate the conversation, which she always did. A few times, she got distracted for a day or so and wondered if the exchange would die out altogether, but then she'd think of something funny to tell him or she'd see a picture on the Internet that was relevant to their conversation, and they'd start up again. She still didn't know much about him, because they never talked about anything personal, but when they landed two or three good jokes in a row there was a kind of exhilaration to it, as if they were dancing.

Then, one night during reading period, she was complaining about how all the dining halls were closed and there was no food in her room because her roommate had raided her care package, and he offered to buy her some Red Vines to sustain her. At first, she deflected this with another joke, because she really did have to study, but he said, *No, I'm serious, stop fooling around and come now,* so she put a jacket over her pajamas and met him at the 7-Eleven.

It was about eleven o'clock. He greeted her without

ceremony, as though he saw her every day, and took her inside to choose some snacks. The store didn't have Red Vines, so he bought her a Cherry Coke Slurpee and a bag of Doritos and a novelty lighter shaped like a frog with a cigarette in its mouth.

"Thank you for my presents," she said, when they were back outside. Robert was wearing a rabbit-fur hat that came down over his ears and a thick, old-fashioned down jacket. She thought it was a good look for him, if a little dorky; the hat heightened his lumberjack aura, and the heavy coat hid his belly and the slightly sad slump of his shoulders.

"You're welcome, concession-stand girl," he said, though of course he knew her name by then. She thought he was going to go in for a kiss and prepared to duck and offer him her cheek, but instead of kissing her on the mouth he took her by the arm and kissed her gently on the forehead, as though she were something precious. "Study hard, sweetheart," he said. "I will see you soon."

On the walk back to her dorm, she was filled with a sparkly lightness that she recognized as the sign of an incipient crush.

While she was home over break, they texted nearly non-stop, not only jokes but little updates about their days. They started saying good morning and good night, and when she asked him a question and he didn't respond right away she felt a jab of anxious yearning. She learned that Robert had two cats, named Mu and Yan, and together

they invented a complicated scenario in which her child-
hood cat, Pita, would send flirtatious texts to Yan, but
whenever Pita talked to Mu she was formal and cold,
because she was jealous of Mu's relationship with Yan.

"Why are you texting all the time?" Margot's stepdad
asked her at dinner. "Are you having an affair with
someone?"

"Yes," Margot said. "His name is Robert, and I met
him at the movie theatre. We're in love, and we're probably
going to get married."

"Hmm," her stepdad said. "Tell him we have some
questions for him."

My parents are asking about u, Margot texted, and Robert
sent her back a smiley-face emoji whose eyes were hearts.

Orange peels, 1999

When Margot returned to campus, she was eager to see Robert again, but he turned out to be surprisingly hard to pin down. *Sorry, busy week at work,* he replied. *I promise I will c u soon.* Margot didn't like this; it felt as if the dynamic had shifted out of her favor, and when eventually he did ask her to go to a movie she agreed right away.

The movie he wanted to see was playing at the theatre where she worked, but she suggested that they see it at the big multiplex just outside town instead; students didn't go there very often, because you needed to drive. Robert came to pick her up in a muddy white Civic with candy wrappers spilling out of the cup holders. On the drive, he was quieter than she'd expected, and he didn't look at her very much. Before five minutes had gone by, she became wildly uncomfortable, and, as they got on the highway, it occurred to her that he could take her someplace and rape and murder her; she hardly knew anything about him, after all.

Just as she thought this, he said, "Don't worry, I'm not going to murder you," and she wondered if the discomfort in the car was her fault, because she was acting jumpy and nervous, like the kind of girl who thought she was going to get murdered every time she went on a date.

"It's O.K.—you can murder me if you want," she said, and he laughed and patted her knee. But he was still disconcertingly quiet, and all her bubbling attempts at making conversation bounced right off him. At the theatre, he made a joke to the cashier at the concession stand about Red Vines, which fell flat in a way that embarrassed everyone involved, but Margot most of all.

During the movie, he didn't hold her hand or put his arm around her, so by the time they were back in the parking lot she was pretty sure that he had changed his mind about liking her. She was wearing leggings and a sweatshirt, and that might have been the problem. When she got into the car, he'd said, "Glad to see you dressed up for me," which she'd assumed was a joke, but maybe she actually had offended him by not seeming to take the date seriously enough, or something. He was wearing khakis and a button-down shirt.

"So, do you want to go get a drink?" he asked when they got back to the car, as if being polite were an obligation that had been imposed on him. It seemed obvious to Margot that he was expecting her to say no and that, when she did, they wouldn't talk again. That made her sad, not so much because she wanted to continue spending time with him as because she'd had such high expectations for him over break, and it didn't seem fair that things had fallen apart so quickly.

"We could go get a drink, I guess?" she said.

"If you want," he said.

"If you want" was such an unpleasant response that she sat silently in the car until he poked her leg and said, "What are you sulking about?"

"I'm not sulking," she said. "I'm just a little tired."

"I can take you home."

CAT PERSON

"No, I could use a drink, after that movie." Even though it had been playing at the mainstream theatre, the film he'd chosen was a very depressing drama about the Holocaust, so inappropriate for a first date that when he suggested it she said, *Lol r u serious,* and he made some joke about how he was sorry that he'd misjudged her taste and he could take her to a romantic comedy instead.

But now, when she said that about the movie, he winced a little, and a totally different interpretation of the night's events occurred to her. She wondered if perhaps he'd been trying to impress her by suggesting the Holocaust movie, because he didn't understand that a Holocaust movie was the wrong kind of "serious" movie with which to impress the type of person who worked at an artsy movie theatre, the type of person he probably assumed she was. Maybe, she thought, her texting *lol r u serious* had hurt him, had intimidated him and made him feel uncomfortable around her. The thought of this possible vulnerability touched her, and she felt kinder toward him than she had all night.

When he asked her where she wanted to go for a drink, she named the place where she usually hung out, but he made a face and said that it was in the student ghetto and he'd take her somewhere better. They went to a bar she'd never been to, an underground speakeasy type of place, with no sign announcing its presence. There was a line to get inside, and, as they waited, she grew fidgety trying to figure out how to tell him what she needed to tell him, but she couldn't, so when the bouncer asked to see her I.D.

she just handed it to him. The bouncer hardly even looked at it; he just smirked and said, "Yeah, no," and waved her to the side, as he gestured toward the next group of people in line.

Robert had gone ahead of her, not noticing what was playing out behind him. "Robert," she said quietly. But he didn't turn around. Finally, someone in line who'd been paying attention tapped him on the shoulder and pointed to her, marooned on the sidewalk.

She stood, abashed, as he came back over to her. "Sorry!" she said. "This is so embarrassing."

"How old *are* you?" he demanded.

"I'm twenty," she said.

"Oh," he said. "I thought you said you were older."

"I told you I was a sophomore!" she said. Standing outside the bar, having been rejected in front of everyone, was humiliating enough, and now Robert was looking at her as if she'd done something wrong.

"But you did that—what do you call it? That gap year," he objected, as though this were an argument he could win.

"I don't know what to tell you," she said helplessly. "I'm twenty." And then, absurdly, she started to feel tears stinging her eyes, because somehow everything had been ruined and she couldn't understand why this was all so hard.

But, when Robert saw her face crumpling, a kind of magic happened. All the tension drained out of his posture; he stood up straight and wrapped his bearlike arms around her. "Oh, sweetheart," he said. "Oh, honey, it's

O.K., it's all right. Please don't feel bad." She let herself be folded against him, and she was flooded with the same feeling she'd had outside the 7-Eleven—that she was a delicate, precious thing he was afraid he might break. He kissed the top of her head, and she laughed and wiped her tears away.

"I can't believe I'm crying because I didn't get into a bar," she said. "You must think I'm such an idiot." But she knew he didn't think that, from the way he was gazing at her; in his eyes, she could see how pretty she looked, smiling through her tears in the chalky glow of the streetlight, with a few flakes of snow coming down.

He kissed her then, on the lips, for real; he came for her in a kind of lunging motion and practically poured his tongue down her throat. It was a terrible kiss, shockingly bad; Margot had trouble believing that a grown man could possibly be so bad at kissing. It seemed awful, yet somehow it also gave her that tender feeling toward him again, the sense that even though he was older than her, she knew something he didn't.

When he was done kissing her, he took her hand firmly and led her to a different bar, where there were pool tables and pinball machines and sawdust on the floor and no one checking I.D.s at the door. In one of the booths, she saw the grad student who'd been her English T.A. her freshman year.

"Should I get you a vodka soda?" Robert asked, which she thought was maybe supposed to be a joke about the kind of drink college girls liked, though she'd never had a vodka soda. She actually was a little anxious about what to order; at the places she went to, they only carded people at the bar, so the kids who were twenty-one or had good fake I.D.s usually brought pitchers of P.B.R. or Bud Light back to share with the others. She wasn't sure if those brands were ones that Robert would make fun of, so, instead of specifying, she said, "I'll just have a beer."

With the drinks in front of him and the kiss behind him, and also maybe because she had cried, Robert became much more relaxed, more like the witty person she knew through his texts. As they talked, she became increasingly sure that what she'd interpreted as anger or dissatisfaction with her had, in fact, been nervousness, a fear that she wasn't having a good time. He kept coming back to her initial dismissal of the movie, making jokes that glanced off it and watching her closely to see how she responded. He teased her about her highbrow taste, and said how hard it was to impress her because of all the film classes she'd taken, even though he knew she'd taken only one summer class in film. He joked about how she and the other employees at the artsy theatre probably sat around and made fun of the people who went to the mainstream theatre, where they didn't even serve wine, and some of the movies were in IMAX 3-D.

Margot laughed along with the jokes he was making at the expense of this imaginary film-snob version of her, though nothing he said seemed quite fair, since she was the one who'd actually suggested that they see the movie

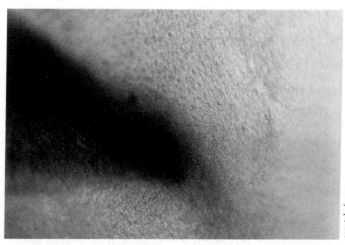

End of lips, 2000

at the Quality 16. Although now, she realized, maybe that had hurt Robert's feelings, too. She'd thought it was clear that she just didn't want to go on a date where she worked, but maybe he'd taken it more personally than that; maybe he'd suspected that she was ashamed to be seen with him. She was starting to think that she understood him—how sensitive he was, how easily he could be wounded—and that made her feel closer to him, and also powerful, because once she knew how to hurt him she also knew how he could be soothed. She asked him lots of questions about the movies he liked, and she spoke self-deprecatingly about the movies at the artsy theatre that she found boring or incomprehensible; she told him about how much her older co-workers intimidated her, and how she sometimes worried that she wasn't smart enough to form her own opinions on anything. The effect of this on him was palpable and immediate, and she felt as if she were petting a large, skittish animal, like a horse or a bear, skillfully coaxing it to eat from her hand.

By her third beer, she was thinking about what it would be like to have sex with Robert. Probably it would be like that bad kiss, clumsy and excessive, but imagining how excited he would be, how hungry and eager to impress her, she felt a twinge of desire pluck at her belly, as distinct and painful as the snap of an elastic band against her skin.

When they'd finished that round of drinks, she said, boldly, "Should we get out of here, then?," and he seemed briefly hurt, as if he thought she was cutting the date short, but she took his hand and pulled him up, and the look on his face when he realized what she was saying, and the obedient way he trailed her out of the bar, gave her that elastic-band snap again, as did, oddly, the fact that his palm was slick beneath hers.

Outside, she presented herself to him again for kissing, but, to her surprise, he only pecked her on the mouth. "You're drunk," he said, accusingly.

"No, I'm not," she said, though she was. She pushed her body against his, feeling tiny beside him, and he let out a great shuddering sigh, as if she were something too bright and painful to look at, and that was sexy, too, being made to feel like a kind of irresistible temptation.

"I'm taking you home, lightweight," he said, shepherding her to the car. Once they were inside it, though, she leaned into him again, and after a little while, by lightly pulling back when he pushed his tongue too far down her throat, she was able to get him to kiss her in the softer way that she liked, and soon after that she was straddling him, and she could feel the small log of his erection straining against his pants. Whenever it rolled beneath her weight, he let out these fluttery, high-pitched moans that she couldn't help feeling were a little melodramatic, and then suddenly he pushed her off him and turned the key in the ignition.

"Making out in the front seat like a teen-ager," he said, in mock disgust. Then he added, "I'd have thought you'd be too old for that, now that you're *twenty*."

She stuck her tongue out at him. "Where do you want to go, then?"

"Your place?"

"Um, that won't really work. Because of my roommate?"

"Oh, right. You live in the dorms," he said, as though that were something she should apologize for.

"Where do you live?" she asked.

"I live in a house."

"Can I . . . come over?"

"You can."

The house was in a pretty, wooded neighborhood not too far from campus and had a string of cheerful white fairy lights across the doorway. Before he got out of the car, he said, darkly, like a warning, "Just so you know, I have cats."

"I know," she said. "We texted about them, remember?"

At the front door, he fumbled with his keys for what seemed a ridiculously long time and swore under his breath. She rubbed his back to try to keep the mood going, but that seemed to fluster him even more, so she stopped.

"Well. This is my house," he said flatly, pushing the door open.

The room they were in was dimly lit and full of objects, all of which, as her eyes adjusted, resolved into familiarity. He had two large, full bookcases, a shelf of vinyl records, a collection of board games, and a lot of art—or, at least, posters that had been hung in frames, instead of being tacked or taped to the wall.

"I like it," she said, truthfully, and, as she did, she identified the emotion she was feeling as relief. It occurred to her that she'd never gone to someone's house to have sex before; because she'd dated only guys her age, there had always been some element of sneaking around, to avoid roommates. It was new, and a little frightening, to be so completely on someone else's turf, and the fact that Robert's house gave evidence of his having interests that she shared, if only in their broadest categories—art, games, books, music—struck her as a reassuring endorsement of her choice.

As she thought this, she saw that Robert was watching her closely, observing the impression the room had made.

And, as though fear weren't quite ready to release its hold on her, she had the brief wild idea that maybe this was not a room at all but a trap meant to lure her into the false belief that Robert was a normal person, a person like her, when in fact all the other rooms in the house were empty, or full of horrors: corpses or kidnap victims or chains. But then he was kissing her, throwing her bag and their coats on the couch and ushering her into the bedroom, groping her ass and pawing at her chest, with the avid clumsiness of that first kiss.

The bedroom wasn't empty, though it was emptier than the living room; he didn't have a bed frame, just a mattress and a box spring on the floor. There was a bottle of whiskey on his dresser, and he took a swig from it, then handed it to her and kneeled down and opened his laptop, an action that confused her, until she understood that he was putting on music.

Margot sat on the bed while Robert took off his shirt and unbuckled his pants, pulling them down to his ankles before realizing that he was still wearing his shoes and bending over to untie them. Looking at him like that, so awkwardly bent, his belly thick and soft and covered with hair, Margot recoiled. But the thought of what it would take to stop what she had set in motion was overwhelming; it would require an amount of tact and gentleness that she felt was impossible to summon. It wasn't that she was scared he would try to force her to do something against her will but that insisting that they stop now, after

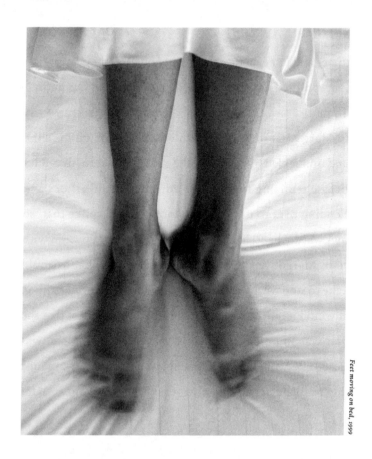

Feet moving on bed, 1999

everything she'd done to push this forward, would make her seem spoiled and capricious, as if she'd ordered something at a restaurant and then, once the food arrived, had changed her mind and sent it back.

She tried to bludgeon her resistance into submission by taking a sip of the whiskey, but when he fell on top of her with those huge, sloppy kisses, his hand moving mechanically across her breasts and down to her crotch, as if he were making some perverse sign of the cross, she began to have trouble breathing and to feel that she really might not be able to go through with it after all.

Wriggling out from under the weight of him and straddling him helped, as did closing her eyes and remembering him kissing her forehead at the 7-Eleven. Encouraged by her progress, she pulled her shirt up over her head. Robert reached up and scooped her breast out of her bra, so that it jutted half in and half out of the cup, and rolled her nipple between his thumb and forefinger. This was uncomfortable, so she leaned forward, pushing herself into his hand. He got the hint and tried to undo her bra, but he couldn't work the clasp, his evident frustration reminiscent of his struggle with the keys, until at last he said, bossily, "Take that thing off," and she complied.

The way he looked at her then was like an exaggerated version of the expression she'd seen on the faces of all the guys she'd been naked with, not that there were that many—six in total, Robert made seven. He looked stunned and stupid with pleasure, like a milk-drunk baby, and she thought that maybe this was what she loved most about sex—a guy revealed like that. Robert showed her more open need than any of the others, even though he was older, and must have seen more breasts, more bodies, than they had—but maybe that was part of it for him, the fact that he was older, and she was young.

As they kissed, she found herself carried away by a fantasy of such pure ego that she could hardly admit even to herself that she was having it. Look at this beautiful girl, she imagined him thinking. She's so perfect, her body is perfect, everything about her is perfect, she's only twenty years old, her skin is flawless, I want her so badly, I want her more than I've ever wanted anyone else, I want her so bad I might die.

The more she imagined his arousal, the more turned-on she got, and soon they were rocking against each other, getting into a rhythm, and she reached into his underwear and took his penis in her hand and felt the pearled droplet of moisture on its tip. He made that sound again, that high-pitched feminine whine, and she wished there were a way she could ask him not to do that, but she couldn't think of any. Then his hand was inside her underwear, and when he felt that she was wet he visibly relaxed. He fingered her a little, very softly, and she bit her lip and put on a show for him, but then he poked her too hard and she flinched, and he jerked his hand away. "Sorry!" he said.

And then he asked, urgently, "Wait. Have you ever done this before?"

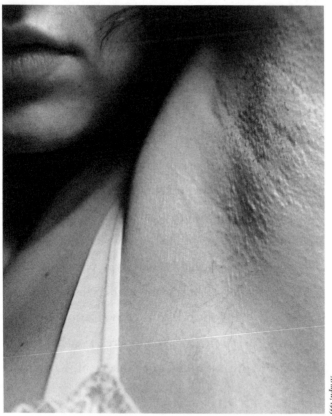

Armpit, 1995

CAT PERSON

The night did, indeed, feel so odd and unprecedented that her first impulse was to say no, but then she realized what he meant and she laughed out loud.

She didn't mean to laugh; she knew well enough already that, while Robert might enjoy being the subject of gentle, flirtatious teasing, he was not a person who would enjoy being laughed at, not at all. But she couldn't help it. Losing her virginity had been a long, drawn-out affair preceded by several months' worth of intense discussion with her boyfriend of two years, plus a visit to the gynecologist and a horrifically embarrassing but ultimately incredibly meaningful conversation with her mom, who, in the end, had not only reserved her a room at a bed-and-breakfast but, after the event, written her a card. The idea that, instead of that whole involved, emotional process, she might have watched a pretentious Holocaust movie, drunk three beers, and then gone to some random house to lose her virginity to a guy she'd met at a movie theatre was so funny that suddenly she couldn't stop laughing, though the laughter had a slightly hysterical edge.

"I'm sorry," Robert said coldly. "I didn't know."

Abruptly, she stopped giggling.

"No, it was . . . nice of you to check," she said. "I've had sex before, though. I'm sorry I laughed."

"You don't need to apologize," he said, but she could tell by his face, as well as by the fact that he was going soft beneath her, that she did.

"I'm sorry," she said again, reflexively, and then, in a burst of inspiration, "I guess I'm just nervous, or something?"

He narrowed his eyes at her, as though suspicious of this claim, but it seemed to placate him. "You don't have to be nervous," he said. "We'll take it slow."

Yeah, right, she thought, and then he was on top of her again, kissing her and weighing her down, and she knew that her last chance of enjoying this encounter had disappeared, but that she would carry through with it until it was over. When Robert was naked, rolling a condom onto a dick that was only half visible beneath the hairy shelf of his belly, she felt a wave of revulsion that she thought might actually break through her sense of pinned stasis, but then he shoved his finger in her again, not at all gently this time, and she imagined herself from above, naked and spread-eagled with this fat old man's finger inside her, and her revulsion turned to self-disgust and a humiliation that was a kind of perverse cousin to arousal.

During sex, he moved her through a series of positions with brusque efficiency, flipping her over, pushing her around, and she felt like a doll again, as she had outside the 7-Eleven, though not a precious one now—a doll made of rubber, flexible and resilient, a prop for the movie that was playing in his head. When she was on top, he slapped her thigh and said, "Yeah, yeah, you like that," with an intonation that made it impossible to tell whether he meant it as a question, an observation, or an order, and when he turned her over he growled in her ear, "I always wanted to fuck a girl with nice tits," and she had to smother her face in the pillow to keep from laughing again. At the end, when he was on top of her in missionary, he kept losing his erection, and every time he did he would say, aggressively, "You make my dick so hard," as though lying about it could make it true. At last, after a frantic rabbity burst, he shuddered, came, and collapsed on her like a tree falling, and, crushed beneath him, she thought, brightly, This is the worst life decision I have ever made! And she marvelled at herself for a while, at the mystery of this person who'd just done this bizarre, inexplicable thing.

After a short while, Robert got up and hurried to the bath-room in a bow-legged waddle, clutching the condom to keep it from falling off. Margot lay on the bed and stared at the ceiling, noticing for the first time that there were stickers on it, those little stars and moons that were supposed to glow in the dark.

Robert returned from the bathroom and stood silhouetted in the doorway. "What do you want to do now?" he asked her.

"We should probably just kill ourselves," she imagined saying, and then she imagined that somewhere, out there in the universe, there was a boy who would think that this moment was just as awful yet hilarious as she did, and that sometime, far in the future, she would tell the boy this story. She'd say, "And then he said, 'You make my dick so hard,'" and the boy would shriek in agony and grab her leg, saying, "Oh, my God, stop, please, no, I can't take it anymore," and the two of them would collapse into each other's arms and laugh and laugh—but of course there was no such future, because no such boy existed, and never would.

So instead she shrugged, and Robert said, "We could watch a movie," and he went to the computer and downloaded something; she didn't pay attention to what. For some reason, he'd chosen a movie with subtitles, and she kept closing her eyes, so she had no idea what was going on. The whole time, he was stroking her hair and trailing light kisses down her shoulder, as if he'd forgotten that ten minutes ago he'd thrown her around as if they were in a porno and growled, "I always wanted to fuck a girl with nice tits" in her ear.

Then, out of nowhere, he started talking about his feelings for her. He talked about how hard it had been

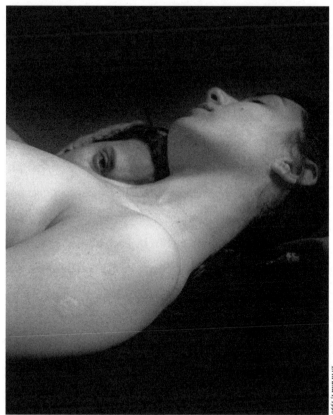

Erin and I, 1998

for him when she went away for break, not knowing if she had an old high-school boyfriend she might reconnect with back home. During those two weeks, it turned out, an entire secret drama had played out in his head, one in which she'd left campus committed to him, to Robert, but at home had been drawn back to the high-school guy, who, in Robert's mind, was some kind of brutish, handsome jock, not worthy of her but nonetheless seductive by virtue of his position at the top of the hierarchy back home in Saline. "I was so worried you might, like, make a bad decision and things would be different between us when you got back," he said. "But I should have trusted you." My high-school boyfriend is gay, Margot imagined telling him. We were pretty sure of it in high school, but after a year of sleeping around at college he's definitely figured it out. In fact, he's not even a hundred per cent positive that he identifies as a man anymore; we spent a lot of time over break talking about what it would mean for him to come out as non-binary, so sex with him wasn't going to happen, and you could have asked me about that if you were worried; you could have asked me about a lot of things. But she didn't say any of that; she just lay silently, emanating a black, hateful aura, until finally Robert trailed off. "Are you still awake?" he asked, and she said yes, and he said, "Is everything O.K.?"

"How old are you, exactly?" she asked him.

"I'm thirty-four," he said. "Is that a problem?"

She could sense him in the dark beside her vibrating with fear.

"No," she said. "It's fine."

"Good," he said. "It was something I wanted to bring up with you, but I didn't know how you'd take it." He rolled over and kissed her forehead, and she felt like a slug he'd poured salt on, disintegrating under that kiss.

She looked at the clock; it was nearly three in the morning. "I should go home, probably," she said.

"Really?" he said. "But I thought you'd stay over. I make great scrambled eggs!"

"Thanks," she said, sliding into her leggings. "But I can't. My roommate would be worried. So."

"Gotta get back to the dorm room," he said, voice dripping with sarcasm.

"Yep," she said. "Since that's where I live."

The drive was endless. The snow had turned to rain. They didn't talk. Eventually, Robert switched the radio to late-night NPR. Margot recalled how, when they first got on the highway to go to the movie, she'd imagined that Robert might murder her, and she thought, Maybe he'll murder me now.

He didn't murder her. He drove her to her dorm. "I had a really nice time tonight," he said, unbuckling his seat belt.

"Thanks," she said. She clutched her bag in her hands. "Me, too."

"I'm so glad we finally got to go on a date," he said.

"*A date*," she said to her imaginary boyfriend. "He called that a *date*." And they both laughed and laughed.

"You're welcome," she said. She reached for the door

handle. "Thanks for the movie and stuff."

"Wait," he said, and grabbed her arm. "Come here." He dragged her back, wrapped his arms around her, and pushed his tongue down her throat one last time. "Oh, my God, when will it end?" she asked the imaginary boyfriend, but the imaginary boyfriend didn't answer her.

"Good night," she said, and then she opened the door and escaped. By the time she got to her room, she already had a text from him: no words, just hearts and faces with heart eyes and, for some reason, a dolphin.

She slept for twelve hours, and when she woke up she ate waffles in the dining hall and binge-watched detective shows on Netflix and tried to envision the hopeful possibility that he would disappear without her having to do anything, that somehow she could just wish him away. When the next message from him did arrive, just after dinner, it was a harmless joke about Red Vines, but she deleted it immediately, overwhelmed with a skin-crawling loathing that felt vastly disproportionate to anything he had actually done. She told herself that she owed him at least some kind of breakup message, that to ghost on him would be inappropriate, childish, and cruel. And, if she did try to ghost, who knew how long it would take him to get the hint? Maybe the messages would keep coming and coming; maybe they would never end.

She began drafting a message—*Thank you for the nice time but I'm not interested in a relationship right now*—but she kept hedging and apologizing, attempting to close loopholes that she imagined him trying to slip through (*It's O.K., I'm not interested in a relationship either, something casual is fine!*), so that the message got longer and longer and even more impossible to send. Meanwhile, his texts kept arriving, none of them saying anything of consequence, each one more earnest than the last. She imagined him lying on his bed that was just a mattress, carefully crafting each one. She remembered that he'd talked a lot about his cats and yet she hadn't seen any cats in the house, and she wondered if he'd made them up.

Every so often, over the next day or so, she would find herself in a gray, daydreamy mood, missing something, and she'd realize that it was Robert she missed, not the real Robert but the Robert she'd imagined on the other end of all those text messages during break.

Hey, so it seems like you're really busy, huh? Robert finally wrote, three days after they'd fucked, and she knew that this was the perfect opportunity to send her half-completed breakup text, but instead she wrote back, *Haha sorry yeah* and *I'll text you soon,* and then she thought, Why did I do that? And she truly didn't know.

"Just tell him you're not interested!" Margot's roommate, Tamara, screamed in frustration after Margot had spent an hour on her bed, dithering about what to say to Robert.

"I have to say more than that. We had *sex*," Margot said.

"*Do* you?" Tamara said. "I mean, really?"

"He's a nice guy, sort of," Margot said, and she wondered how true that was. Then, abruptly, Tamara lunged, snatching the phone out of Margot's hand and holding it far away from her as her thumbs flew across the screen. Tamara flung the phone onto the bed and Margot scrambled for it, and there it was, what Tamara had written: *Hi im not interested in you stop textng me.*

"Oh, my God," Margot said, finding it suddenly hard to breathe.

"What?" Tamara said boldly. "What's the big deal? It's true."

But they both knew that it was a big deal, and Margot had a knot of fear in her stomach so solid that she thought she might retch. She imagined Robert picking up his phone, reading that message, turning to glass, and shattering to pieces.

"Calm down. Let's go get a drink," Tamara said, and they went to a bar and shared a pitcher, and all the while Margot's phone sat between them on the table, and though they tried to ignore it, when it chimed with an incoming message they screamed and clutched each other's arms.

"I can't do it—you read it," Margot said. She pushed the phone toward Tamara. "You did this. It's your fault."

But all the message said was *O.K., Margot, I am sorry to hear that. I hope I did not do anything to upset you. You are a sweet girl and I really enjoyed the time we spent together. Please let me know if you change your mind.*

Margot collapsed on the table, laying her head in her hands. She felt as though a leech, grown heavy and swollen with her blood, had at last popped off her skin, leaving a tender, bruised spot behind. But why should she feel that way? Perhaps she was being unfair to Robert, who really had done nothing wrong, except like her, and be bad in bed, and maybe lie about having cats, although probably they had just been in another room.

But then, a month later, she saw him in the bar—her bar, the one in the student ghetto, where, on their date, she'd suggested they go. He was alone, at a table in the back, and he wasn't reading or looking at his phone; he was just sitting there silently, hunched over a beer.

She grabbed the friend she was with, a guy named Albert. "Oh, my God, that's him," she whispered. "The guy from the movie theatre!" By then, Albert had heard a version of the story, though not quite the true one; nearly all her friends had. Albert stepped in front of her, shielding her from Robert's view, as they rushed back to the table where their friends were. When Margot announced that Robert was there, everyone erupted in astonishment, and then they surrounded her and hustled her out of the bar as if she were the President and they were the Secret Service. It was all so over-the-top that she wondered if she was acting like a mean girl, but, at the same time, she truly did feel sick and scared.

CAT PERSON

Curled up on her bed with Tamara that night, the glow of the phone like a campfire illuminating their faces, Margot read the messages as they arrived:

Hi Margot, I saw you out at the bar tonight. I know you said not to text you but I just wanted to say you looked really pretty. I hope you're doing well!

I know I shouldnt say this but I really miss you

hey maybe I don't have the right to ask but I just wish youd tell me what it is I did wrog
*wrong

I felt like we had a real connection did you not feel that way or . . .

CAT PERSON

Maybe I was too old for u or maybe you liked someone else

Is that guy you were with tonight your boyfriend

???

Or is he just some guy you are fucking

Sorry

When u laguehd when I asked if you were a virgin was it because youd fucked so many guys

Are you fucking that guy right now

CAT PERSON

Are you

Are you

Are you

Are you

Are you

Answer me

Whore.

ELINOR CARUCCI's photographs have been exhibited worldwide, including at the Museum of Modern Art in New York and the Gagosian Gallery in London. A Guggenheim Fellow, Carucci was commissioned by the *New Yorker* to capture the image that accompanied Kristen Roupenian's *Cat Person* when it appeared in the magazine. She is represented by Edwynn Houk Gallery.

KRISTEN ROUPENIAN'S DEBUT COLLECTION
COMING FEBRUARY 2019